TALKING AMONGST MYSELF

PUBLICATIONS

The Gate

Rowan Grainger Paintings

The Divine Springtime - Paintings

Colours Rising

Talking Amongst Myself

For Sam, Simon and Abe.

And with thanks to Juliet for the books

TALKING AMONGST MYSELF

Reflections of an artist.
Chris Rowan Grainger

The Rehearsal

CONTENTS

MR PRANGLEY

Even though I had lived there for many years, it always amazed me how long and far down hill you had to walk to reach the centre of Bath which is in a natural crater. Looking for number thirty-one, I was walking along a narrow lane of small Georgian cottages high above the city which spread out below me with its tiny roofs and steeples.

This was another stranger for me to visit as I searched for a cure for my son's breathing problems. This could be awkward and embarrassing. If this man I had never met turned out to be a bogus healer, or worse, if he had mental problems I had no defence except retreat. I did not fear mental handicap – it was mental illness I was always so poor at handling.

A black door with no bell, but an unpolished brass knocker. After a brief wait, when the door opened, a dark grey suit appeared. It was the unexpected suit I noticed first, rather than the thin man wearing it. He took me from the street into a long, slim room which made me think of a good quality Victorian railway carriage. There was a feeling of shiny mahogany and substantially framed watercolours on the walls, but most extraordinary of all, at eye-level, there was a conglomeration of objects I had never experienced before and never shall again: A globe of the earth about the size of a football and surrounding it, through eight coloured crystals, shone eight small spotlights, focusing their beams onto different parts of the Earth.

"I was a jeweller for many years, I had my own business," said the slender man from inside the suit.

Not feeling ready or prepared to ask questions about his strange well- engineered contraption I changed the subject.

"We were wondering if there was anything you could do to help my son's breathing. Not a chest problem, a nasal one."

Without a pause for thought, and with reassuring confidence he replied,

"Yes certainly we can. Gem Stone Healing is very good for all sorts of Asthma and breathing problems. We'll put his name on the International Link. We have even healed A.I.D.S."

I noticed the "We," and wondered if there were other individuals in suits lurking in other rooms of the house with equally strange contraptions.

"What is The International Link?" I enquired.

"This," he said, taking me over to the spot-lit globe. "We'll put his name here, which will strengthen his immune system."

There seemed to be no pomposity or guile in Mr Prangley while he proposed these highly improbable cures. Here was a man in his late sixties, though he could have been much older, tidily dressed in his dark grey suit, as if on the way to work in a bank. He showed me this strange piece of equipment as if it belonged quite naturally to an NHS surgery.

"And Gem Stone Healing?" I queried.

"Gems." He echoed, "Passing light through special stones. I pioneered it and developed it from my work as a jeweller. It has great benefit to the human tissue, as you can imagine."

Yes I can imagine, I thought. I can imagine all sorts of things – pigs driving aeroplanes, cows trampolening on the moon, but many things exist only in the imagination. How easy it is for complementary healers of all descriptions to promise an improvement to a condition as long as you follow their advice: Banana Pulp Immersion, Yankse Mud Pills, Cumbrian Fire Walking. As long as the promise is made with confidence and a brief tale of success it is hard for the average desperate customer to oppose it. Easier to stand there as a wholly impressionable, even grateful, client. Gems are nice, light is cheerful. Put the two together and you could heal the world - voila!

My difficulty was that Mr Prangley, being so absolutely certain about everything, sent me into a trance. Out there was a world of maybe and perhaps. Inside his first-class railway compartment all doubts were put aside and Mr Certainty prevailed.

"I invented Tupperware," he said.

"You? Tupperware?" I said, sounding like the recitative for a soap opera.

"Oh yes, it was my invention."

What a strange thing for a jeweller to invent, I thought. Tupperware not being on my list of cultural experiences, and therefore having no appropriate reply to hand, I tried hard to look at its esteemed inventor with the correct portion of admiration. Then, probably trying to throw out a grappling hook to regain my own familiar world, I completely changed the subject. Trying to match Mr Prangley's good manners I said,

"I hope you don't mind me saying this, but your pictures look very interesting."

"Yes, my pictures, many of them are very special."

"This one looks rather like a John Sell Cotman," I said – "light shapes against a dark background."

He went over to a small oil painting of a young boy writing something in a dark interior as if he was doing schoolwork.

"I'm sure this is a Walter Sickert. It's not signed, that's the pity of it," he said. "The wretched valuers, the saleroom people, doubt everything that's not signed, but I'm sure it's a Sickert. I just wish I could find someone to do some research on it."

Pictures and artworks being much more in my line of interest than Tupperware, I found myself in London a few weeks later with a photo of Mr Prangley's Sickert in my hand, sorting through the Walter Sickert files at the Courtauld Institute in the Strand to see if I could find any pictures with a resemblance to the boy in the schoolroom. But unfortunately I had to return to the art collector without any great news, and feeling sorry to disappoint him. The boy in the schoolroom remained an orphan without a creator. The Gem Stone Healer now showed me a beautifully illustrated manuscript depicting the letter G surrounding a colourfully dressed gathering of twelve disciples adoring the mother of Jesus who was hovering in the air above them.

"I am sure this is a Mantegna," he said. "I've researched it and it is exactly his style. I can't see how it can be by anybody else. Of course, without a signature, the devils in the big salerooms will disagree with me."

It was refreshing to see Mr Prangley's certainty about the provenance of his collection return after the Sickert disappointment. I admired his Mantegna, whoever painted it. It was a beautiful, entertaining little thing not much more than six inches square. It was during this visit that he also showed me, among other paintings, his Russian Icon, dark and ancient. It depicted the Saviour and three saints, two of them female. The picture looked so old that, while the faces were intact, some body parts were missing, their incompleteness seeming to endorse their authenticity and age. I could imagine the smoke from many years of church candles slowly turning the icon a leathery brown.

But hadn't I originally visited Gordon Prangley to seek a cure for my son's breathing problems, rather than for a discourse on art? I decided to use myself as an experiment – a practice run to test the Gem Stone Healing, to experience what my son might have to endure if we decided to go through with it. So a week or so after what I mistakenly understood to be the definitive and final art tour of the room, when I thought I had seen all of Mr Prangley's collection, I lay on a narrow bed similar to one which a masseur might use, feeling as if I was about to be propelled into space. This particular black Rexine bed was clean but had an antique feel to it, as if it might have been lain upon by other devotees of the works of Mantegna, Cotman and Russian Icons. Lesser enthusiasts might well have made their excuses and left at an earlier stage of acquaintance with this bizarre man. A large black metal disc was now lowered from the ceiling to a position parallel and just above my body. Hundreds of coloured stones which looked like rubies, emeralds, amethysts, crystals and others for which I had no name were set into the disc. There was something of the Star Ship in this experience. Would I now be frozen for a thousand years? Is this how an alien abduction starts? I had asked Mr Prangley how many clothes I was to remove before climbing on the bed.

"Oh it works through clothing," he had replied.

What works through clothing? I thought. He switched on the lamps which illuminated all the gems, scattering coloured light onto my thankfully covered body. A Christmas tree fairy might endure a whole season of this. The inventor sat calmly and confidently nearby with his thoughts certainly not on me, but probably planning his next contribution to the needs of the world. It was half an hour before the light was switched off and I was released from my position of supine submissiveness.

"Nothing unpleasant there," I said, trying to be jokey, but feeling relieved. "All those precious stones – very attractive."

"Oh, yes," assured Mr Prangley, "You'll feel the benefit, there's no doubt about that."

A week later I arrived with my son. As we entered the familiar room we found that four men and one woman, all of different ages, all in suits of a similar shade of grey, were sitting near the illuminated globe. They were on settles facing eachother, making me think of a small chapel congregation. Always gentlemanly, Mr Prangley introduced them: "These are my scientific friends, here for a conference."

These friends were totally silent and didn't seem to acknowledge our presence, probably seeing us an interruption.

They were not referred to again and my son was soon under the lights and jewels, as I had been. By the time his session was over, the grey-clad scientific conference near the entrance must have finished because the delegates had all disappeared. Mr Prangley took me over to the lit-up globe where my son's name lay written on a piece of paper.

"We're having to do something about The Greys," he said.

"The Greys?" I queried, with a distant memory that there was an army regiment by that name. I wondered if they were in some sort of danger. Then he pointed to a small realistic illustration of an alien propped up by the globe. Indeed it was a very grey alien with mean pointed features, tiny nostrils and very narrow slitted eyes.

"They are giving us a lot of trouble at the moment, threatening to become a very unpleasant influence in the world."

All this was said with such authority, no doubt strengthened by the recent conference with his scientific friends, that I was speechless again. What, I thought, would be an appropriate reply on the subject of Grey Aliens when they are totally new to you? Best to bow to Mr Prangley's certainty.

"Oh, really?" I said, immediately revealing my total ignorance, and disqualifying myself from any possibility of becoming a scientific friend.

But we were not to leave the house without another artistic revelation, and this one was to be the most extraordinary of all. My eight year old son and I were escorted down a short flight of stairs at the far end of the only room in the house I had yet seen. Here was a lower floor, well lit by a window overlooking Bath. In this room there were four or five large free-standing glazed cabinets, showing a collection of beautifully displayed objects.

"This is my collection of porcelain," said the man of many parts.

I was amazed. This was a beautiful collection: Chinese vases of glorious subtle colour, eastern bowls and plates of perfect proportion. He took out a vase measuring about eighteen inches high.

"This is probably my most interesting piece. It's valuable. It has this lovely blue repeating pattern – Sung Dynasty. The salerooms have a conspiracy, you see. They want to get their hands on my collection for next-to-nothing and then share the proceeds between them. It's quite a common procedure. There's one very similar to this in the Percival David Foundation in London."

I looked carefully at it. My inexpert eye was seduced. Whatever anyone said about it, it was truly a thing confident in its beauty. He brought out some small bowls painted with birds in gentle, sensitive colours: pinks and greens and a cloudy blue, showing me the markings underneath and the quality of the glazes. Then he took out another vase, pale turquoise, showing me the particular crackleture webbing across the surface.

"The only other one known is in the British Museum," he said. "They know this one's here."

By "they" I understood him to mean the people in the museum, not the mean-faced, slit-eyed aliens. Being highly impressed by this painstakingly assembled and beautiful collection, and wanting to do something to help Mr Prangley resolve its value, I said:

"I know the local representative of Galloway's. He will come to your house to value things. He valued a painting and a drawing I had. He seemed fair, and the painting got a good price at auction. The drawing I decided to keep."

Normally quick and sharp, this time he took a little while to think about what I had said. Then, seeming to contemplate each word:

"All right then, if you know him, if he can come here, we can see what he says."

"Don't worry," I said, "I'll arrange it and be here to give you some support, if you like."

Before we left, the collector, healer and inventor of Tupperware handed me his little Mantegna painting.

"I want you to have this," he said.

"Me? … Why?" – It's one of your most beautiful things, and you're so fond of it."

"It's for all the things you have done," he said, "That research in London and everything."

"Are you sure?"

"Quite sure." I thanked him, baffled with delight. Mantegna or not, it was a beautiful thing and I would cherish it. I didn't believe I had done anything to deserve it. I had just shown an interest, that's all.

Two weeks later I was in the china room again with Gordon Prangley and Henry Tailgroth, Area Representative for Galloway's international Salerooms, who had arrived just before me to assess the art collection and porcelain. He was a tall man of the hunting and fishing variety, dressed in browns and greens as if camouflaged in the event of a high street encounter with a herd of antelope or wild boar. He looked into each showcase, taking out a bowl here, a plate there, turning them over without enthusiasm. I noticed that he didn't touch either of the vases as if he had made up his mind already. He made a short call to head office about one of the small bowls painted with birds.

This was the same man who had come to my home not very long before, and given me a completely correct and fair assessment of a 1930s watercolour portrait. He had shown me politeness and consideration, yet here in front of Mr Prangley he showed an insensitive casual arrogance in contrast to this particular collector's restraint and good manners.

At last Tailgroth made his announcement without looking at either of us,

"Things are not always what they appear. There is nothing

here of very much value. They are copies – very good copies, and attractive of course, but I'm afraid a long way from being the real thing."

I could see, though he said nothing, Gordon Prangley was utterly stunned. He remained calm. Then, breaking the tragic silence, I said impetuously,

"Mr Prangley is the most enthusiastic person in the world and it has been a pleasure knowing him."

I can't remember whether the Galloway's man left the house before me. He probably did because, as a further act of generosity, I was also given the Russian Icon which, together with the Mantegna I still live with very happily.

A little while later I learnt from a mutual acquaintance that Mr Prangley had died suddenly of a stroke. It must have been shortly after the valuation, when all the confidence and certainty would have been drained from the house. He was surely more committed and energised by his art collection than all his Tupperware creation and gem stones put together. It was even more important to him than the elimination of the Greys. The importance of his collection gave his life a central purpose. Then on that one critical morning its worth was taken away.

Years later I had the Icon and the Mantegna examined as a matter of interest. The first, though badly damaged, was certainly Russian and from the nineteenth century. Mr Prangley's Mantegna turned out to be a Victorian copy of a Renaissance illuminated manuscript.

"You can tell by the faces," said the saleroom expert, "Each period paints faces according to the current fashion, they can't help it. These are Victorian faces – do you see what I mean?"

Yes I saw what he meant but I am delighted to have it hanging in my bedroom – the joint enthusiasm of an artist and a collector. And that certainty makes it rare enough for me. My son eventually grew out of his breathing difficulties;

no harm done by all those illuminated jewels. As for the Greys, perhaps they are still with us, or perhaps they have moved on, feeding only on enthusiasm.

THE VACANT PLINTH
IN TRAFALGAR SQUARE

A little woman standing on a huge stone block was attempting to attract the attention of bored passers-by. How tiny we really are was illustrated to me when I happened to be in Trafalgar Square and witnessed the artistic project allowing real human beings onto the vacant stone plinth near the National Gallery. The idea was conceived by Anthony Gormley, famous for his gigantic iron sculpture, 'Angel of the North.' He said that it would be novel, thought-provoking and socially unifying to put a series of real people on the plinth for an hour each. There was no shortage of volunteers. Anyone could apply on-line and do whatever they wanted on the stone block as long as it was lawful. He also thought it would be 'challenging' which seems to be the general ambition of the current art world, but I'm not sure whether this was, for example, the primary aim of Degas, Seurat or Van Gogh, whose artworks hang only a stone's throw away.

I soon asked myself why the project seemed such an interesting failure. It seemed to me to show more graphically than any essay or discourse the purpose and justification of art. People are the subject of art. They make it. But they are not art objects themselves. They are the source of the light but not the reflectors of that light. The sun cannot be both star and mirror at the same time. It may be said that in the theatre humans themselves are the art-works. But this is not so: they are always reflecting somebody or something outside themselves. Romeo is not the actor but the character the actor is reflecting. Giselle is not the dancer but a personality the dancer inhabits.

A few years ago there was a most unlikely sculpture on that plinth: 'Alison Lapper Pregnant' by Marc Quinn 2005 - a large stone carving of a naked woman with tiny arms and legs (caused by her own mother taking the drug Thalidomide when pregnant) You may think, as I did when I read about it beforehand, what a grotesque idea for a sculpture – particularly as the model for the carving was a real woman, and not an imaginary one. But the beautiful pure white marble, rounded forms of the body and the profound nobility of her face looking out across Trafalgar Square, made it one of the most memorable pieces of sculpture I have seen. In its way it was as victorious as Admiral Nelson on his column and as brave as the generals on their muscular bronze horses which inhabit the other stone plinths around the famous quadrangle. By comparison, the real live woman I saw standing on that stone block lecturing as large a gathering as she could manage to attract – perhaps a shifting band of six or eight people – on some issue of great importance to her, looked absurd and insignificant, like a small mouse lecturing a herd of grazing cattle.

She was, of course, totally out of scale with the plinth. She hadn't been 'designed' for it. Her purpose was muddled. What was she there for? To engage? To impress the public as the equestrian bronzes do? To celebrate a victory as Nelson does? To inspire human compassion and respect as the naked figure did? Or even to amuse as a comic object might do? No, she was nowhere near any of these things, nor did she have the power to provoke or challenge. She was simply using this great man-made monolith as a platform for her talk, complete with lectern. It was her 'soap-box' when her talk could have been more effectively delivered from a beer crate. I don't know whether all the volunteers preceding her had failed just as dismally, but they could never have been anything but tiny humans standing on a large stone block, their fragility emphasised by a substantial safety net stretched around them on all four sides.

The woman speaker I saw on that day appeared like a fly on a suitcase or an ant on a shoebox. Art is a metaphor for life; a form for discussing an aspect of what it is like to be human, whereas a woman is not a metaphor, she is the source of the metaphor. She is not a piece of sculpture. She can pretend to be, but a piece of sculpture does it better.

A THEORETICAL EXPLANATION OF COINCIDENCES, BASED ON CURRENT SCIENCE

In recent years the physicists studying the Quantum, or sub-atomic world of the very small indeed have discovered ever more sub-divisions of the atom which not very many years ago was thought to be indivisible. Among the very basic building blocks of matter are what are called Quarks, held together with particles called Gluons. There are also Leptons which perform a different function in the atom. These little creations form the very basic structures. Unfortunately things are not as simple as they sound because scientists realise that all this leaves so much still to be explained. Top of the list is that it does not answer the question of gravity – what causes a ball thrown up generally to come down again – nor the reason why particles come together to form particular mass and weight.

So, never short of creative ideas, some physicists have come up with something called Superstring Theory which proposes that all those tiny subdivisions of the atom are not particles at all, but tiny vibrating strands of energy that oscillate in many dimensions, some of which we know about and many we don't, all of which need a lot more knowledge and understanding.

Coincidences or co-incidents - unexpected and unlikely connections between events - are much more interesting than just being chance happenings. They are more easily explained if we can manage to alter our accustomed view of the universe from one occupied by solid objects to one where everything, from tree to toenail, is really, in essence, a vibration. Our perception of the world being solid is really a false one; a musical, vibrational world would be nearer the truth.

Coincidences come about when we, who have our own vibrational 'wavelengths', come into a state of harmony with the vibration of another person or event or idea which is in sympathy with our point of interest at that moment. In other words, coincidences happen when vibrations of which we are made harmonise with other vibrations outside ourselves, causing attraction. For example: two people have spent time rehearsing a particular piece of music. On coming out of the practice room they go to the car, switch on the radio and out comes the same piece of music they have just been working on. This could be explained by the musicians, vibrating at a certain frequency connected with the tune then connect to the same frequency being transmitted by the radio station at the same moment. These vibrations attract each other .

The musical harmony or disharmony between ourselves and the world around us is happening all the time in a perpetual connection between all things, but we only notice the particularly unusual connections because they take us by surprise and we call them coincidences, or a popular word, serendipity.

Made as we are and conditioned by our perception of solidity it is difficult for us to visualise the musical, harmonic fundamentals of things, but, consciously or subconsciously we frequently tune in to other vibrations which connect to the ones with which we are involved at a particular moment.

How many times have we heard people say when someone contacts them or suddenly appears unexpectedly,

'Oh, I was just thinking about you!'

A way to imagine it might be to think of tuning in to a radio programme or finding a website which has a similar subject matter to the one we are concentrating on, but instead of twiddling knobs or a mouse, it is being done automatically by the vibrations of our subconscious so, because we don't seem to have taken any action to bring it about, we are amazed.

But the radio and computer images are extremely crude compared to the complex beauty of the multi-dimensional vibrations which comprise our universe, of which we are a linked and inseparable part.

Superstring theory is by no means fixed. It leaves many physicists unconvinced because of its failure to encompass all the questions of science, particularly those of gravity and mass. Also, at the quantum, subatomic level of science, experiments to prove a hypothesis are extremely difficult, not least because mini particles and waves behave differently when they are being observed from when they are not, as if they are playing a constant and light-hearted game of 'Now You See Me, Now You Don't.'

However it is only a question of time before much more is understood . Science seldom remains static for very long. By the end of the twenty-first century we may be at a point where 'coincidences' could be much more under our control because a way towards understanding these fundamental vibrations will have been discovered. We will probably be much nearer to using harmonic vibrations for the benefit and development of the human race. An area at present occupied by clairvoyants, psychics, spiritual healers and the religious at prayer will be inhabited by everyone, and could well be accepted into conventional medical practice.

However, humanity and scientific exploration have a long way to develop before this can come about. Meanwhile those who talk of 'Good Vibrations', or even of 'Bad Vibes' are probably thinking in the right direction. In each case of coincidences we ourselves are the link, the bridge, the spark which unites the two related but hitherto unconnected events. Without ourselves to make meaning and significance out of them they would remain two separate happenings without any link at all, so we voluntarily create the coincidence by reading significance into it. The tune playing in the musicians' heads as they come from rehearsal and the same tune playing on the radio moments later could easily stay utterly separate if unremarked upon, or picked up on, by one of the people involved.

The Actress

SOME THOUGHTS ON ACTING

When I was lucky enough to find myself on a two year acting course at the Bristol Old Vic School in 1957, run at that time by the outstanding teacher Duncan Ross, the method by which he trained actors was this:

'Every line that is spoken, or body movement made on stage, is done in order to do something to another person; to bring about some effect on another character, however insignificant that effect might be.' So the constant question was: 'What are you trying to do?'

Although this approach served its purpose up to a point; it encouraged eye contact between actors for example, and it brought about, often, a passable feeling of reality, I know Duncan Ross himself was not totally happy with it. He told me that it was a method he had come to after many years in the theatre, and in the process of teaching it was a tool he used for his work.

It was, however too clever for me, not encouraging enough commitment and conviction. For example, the line:

"My Lord, the carriage has arrived bearing Lady Pendlehurst and her daughter Mary,"
has to be worked on before we can be sure what it is we are actually trying to do. And it is not earth-shattering after all, when the work is done.

The soliloquies in Hamlet are good examples of this difficulty. What is Hamlet trying to do to anyone with

"To be, or not to be. That is the question.?"

He is probably trying to work something out for himself which could make him reluctant to share it with others. Or, more probably, he is sharing his thoughts directly with the audience?

The challenge: "What is he trying to do?" is too subtle, too intellectual. So what would be a better approach?

I am now at an age when I have seen enough productions to be able to make a reasonable evaluation of different performances. When we are young we have little experience to compare one acting performance with another, so when we are asked:

"What did you think of Michael Doings in 'The Last Stand of Dood?" we cannot really answer convincingly, because it is not possible to know how someone else might have played it. We have not enough experience to compare one thing with another. If we are not careful we might answer:
"I read Tony Bluster in The Times and he liked it very much." This is not answering the question.

But, many hundreds of plays and films later, we can begin to see what stands out from the rest. We may call a performance good acting because we find it particularly convincing and moving compared with other performances we have seen.

Of course, when we are young and inexperienced, we can honestly say whether or not something we see affects us deeply or makes us laugh. Later on, with more experience, we can express how exceptional a performance is by comparing it to others we have seen.

So, I have come to the conclusion that good acting is simply about utter conviction. It is about saying a line - any line- as if it is the most important line ever. Only then will the audience be convinced and really interested.

The eminent theatre director Peter Brook said recently on Radio 4,

"An actor has to believe every word he says, otherwise he is unbelievable."

Imagine saying the above line:

"My Lord, the carriage has arrived bearing Lady Pendlehurst and her daughter Mary" as if it really, really mattered. How interesting it could be.

Try thinking of a real cliché; one that you find very boring when it is spoken. How about:

'Long time no see!'

Try saying it ordinarily, and then say it as if it is the most important thing you can think of; the most important thing you have ever had to say. By this approach an utterance of unspeakable dullness, completely lacking in originality, can be turned into a line worth listening to.

Great comedy actors do this all the time. Often their lines on the page are not funny at all; it is the conviction with which they are said that makes them hilarious. Eric Morecambe and Ernie Wise were a good example of this. Many of their lines were very ordinary, but they made them extraordinary by giving them a hugely unexpected importance, as if their whole lives depended on what they were saying.

Now we must look at the question of style. It might be said that this theory of mine could be good for pantomime or comedy. But when we come to realism lines should be delivered in the same way as they are said in real life. Style is extremely important in drama. You cannot successfully play Noel Coward and Anton Checkov in the same way. One is formal, funny and needs mechanical precision. The other is contemplative, funny and poetic, but all the time realistic. Pantomime suffers nowadays because television performers, used to appearing close to cameras, are suddenly, when cast for a Christmas show and required to throw their lines out to a live audience like parcels of goodies, are unable to do it. If the style is wrong the show feels wrong to the audience, even though they may not know what is being denied them.

If we return to realism and the need to act a play utterly realistically how can theatre be absolutely realistic and interesting at the same time? If we want realistic dialogue we might as well go to the pub and listen to the customers. I believe the answer to this is that lines can be said with absolute conviction and still be realistic. Surely we would rather someone spoke to us as if they really meant what they were saying than as if they did not care. We are bound to receive a more interested response from others if we address them with the feeling that our words are really important. Otherwise, why are we saying them?

The link which holds all this together is conviction. A line said with absolute conviction is what makes an actor worth listening to. It would be difficult to imagine a line more boring than:

"I tried a new way this time. I came off the A39 and took the B320 through Seal, which actually passes Grimsby altogether."

But perhaps it could be made <u>thrilling</u> if delivered as if it was the most important information in the world.

DRAWING

The art of drawing – that is, creating the impression of a three dimensional form on a two dimensional surface - is not considered to be a particularly interesting subject just now; partly because visual art has gone on one of its periodical holidays from figurative painting to other media methods of conveying feelings, such as photography and video film, and also because drawing is mostly done in monochrome while we are in an age of colour, however subdued. Nevertheless, the skill of drawing is the basis of all figurative art which, in its turn, is the basis of most of the wonderful visual art throughout the centuries. Also, interestingly, young people are required to be able to draw if they want to achieve good art exam results, so in this area at least drawing is not forgotten. I have often been asked to help students, of a variety of ages, who had spent a long time under the impression that drawing was either an unnecessary skill, or that it was an accomplishment that just came to you after you had been doing art for a couple of years. But neither of these misapprehensions last for very long because when exams or assessments appear over the horizon and the student suddenly realises that none of their drawings are convincing; in fact they look rather flimsy and feeble, these disappointed people often panic and look for help.

Fortunately I have found that they can be helped remarkably easily, and I have seen a student come for a first lesson showing me their best work – a very careful, flat and dull drawing – ending the morning with a really strong and exciting piece of work which at once gives them enormous encouragement and takes pride of place in their portfolio.

People can learn to draw at a very early age. There are

many approaches to drawing, and so there should be. How tedious if everyone drew the same way. In fact I try to encourage individuality from the start so that a student does not for a moment feel they must draw like me. One of my criticisms of art schools would be that teachers often only have time for students who draw in a similar style to themselves. I remember achieving a small pencil nude in a life class. I was quite pleased because I thought it had a lot of energy.

"Too many lines" was the remark of the tutor as he walked past.

I think it is very dull to have a room-full of pictures all done by different people, all looking the same.

There is an approach I have come across through studying the subject over many years which allows for a multitude of different interpretations: I put the emphasis on where the light is coming from. I do this right at the start instead of as an advanced concept. I have found that by seeing an object with light hitting it makes the point immediately that it appears solid, it has weight and therefore is not a flat, stuck on shape with an outline. This is the weakness in most people's early drawing – the subject has no weight.

Now, my approach does not mean that lots of light and dark shading is the criterion of a good drawing – not at all. For example the line drawings of Picasso and Matisse are superb, but this quality is very rare. It is so very rare that even an artist with a lifetime of experience may find it difficult to give an impression of solid weight with just a line. Light is what makes things appear solid and so it is helpful to recognise this when we start to draw.

When we draw objects with a light side and a dark side we see them as having weight and volume, and it is interesting how line soon begins to take care of itself. The opposite approach would be to insist on very accurate line drawings and then, later on, to introduce shading as if it were an inessential addition. But I am not in favour of this way of teaching. I believe it encourages a concept of flatness or 'map drawing' from the start when really the excitement of a drawing comes from the apparent weight and energy of the forms within it, and not from the accuracy of the outline.

When we recognise form as opposed to just line we really start to look at three dimensional things with interest. This is what drawing is after all – looking. Drawing is also the essential ingredient of good painting. Even abstract painting needs an awareness of weight and form, and a feeling for the third dimension. Drawing is the place where we look, we enquire, we try things out and we make mistakes. These are the adventures which can make drawings appear so interesting and personal.

A BRIEF ESSAY ON COMPOSITION IN ART

In connection with painting and sculpture we commonly hear the words 'Line, form and colour.' In the case of sculpture may be added the word 'texture.'

In my half a century of passionate connection with the visual arts I have never heard or read of anyone stressing the importance of composition, or the putting together of a picture. Compositions are admired sometimes, but never with a clear idea of what the word means. I have seen diagrammatic attempts to analyse them – particularly in the case of Leonardo da Vinci's 'The Last Supper' - but these analyses are so complicated that they cannot easily be followed, and I have noticed that another art book might easily contain a very different diagram showing the composition to be constructed in a very different way.

Not long ago I gave a lecture about paintings I specially liked to the Bath Arts Society, and when I mentioned composition and that I had experienced difficulties early on as a painter with the construction of pictures, and that I had taken a long time to discover an approach which released the energy I was looking for, the audience of forty or so, mostly artists themselves, seemed very surprised. I felt they had not really thought much about composition. Either it came completely naturally to them which made them very fortunate, or they just had no need to address it. After my talk one man said to me,

'Composition is one of those things that cannot really be taught.' I disagree. I am sure the early painters were taught approaches to composition, but their conversations have been lost.

David Hockney has spoken some plain common sense on

the subject in his preface to the book 'Pictures by David Hockney,' published by Thames and Hudson:

'Our delight in the pictures is in the way they're constructed; that's what makes them stand out, not the story.'

There is a popular misconception that a big division exists between abstract and figurative art. This is not true. The only difference between them is that figurative art uses symbols which are recognisable as objects or figures in everyday life, whereas abstraction tries hard to avoid using shapes and symbols which we recognise. This is not as easy as it seems because most shapes remind us of something.

Many people think that the construction of a picture, an abstract idea, only belongs to abstract art, whereas the moment figures and objects appear construction takes care of itself, as if the elephant designs the room. It doesn't.

The construction, or composition – the way different parts of a picture are put together to form an energetic whole – is hugely important whatever is being painted or drawn, in whatever style.

I sensed the importance of this when I attempted my very first paintings. Take some boats, for instance, some sea, harbour, sky. Where do you put them on the picture surface? Does it matter? Looking at really great and successful paintings I thought there must be some process, some method or even some basic law which prevents the different components appearing dull and lifeless. It seemed to me that I needed an approach which would unlock the potential energy of a painting by each thing sparking off every other thing; so that all the possible excitement of a painting could be realised. It would be rather like a car running sweetly on all cylinders and brand new spark plugs, or a generator with all its leads properly connected. But where would I start to achieve this? I knew that all great paintings adhere to their own simple plan. You can sense the simple design of, say, Piero della Francesca's 'Nativity' in the National Gallery without knowing what that plan is. To me it was as if great artists keep these things to themselves – a brotherhood which does not share this great secret with anyone except with each other.

I made numerous test drawings in my early sketchbooks which soon appeared to be full of scribbles: First of all I tried three elements or parts of a picture, with each part hopefully sparking off each other part, but this didn't seem enough. Then I tried four, five and six parts to the picture, but I just couldn't quite catch hold of an answer. And where do you start? Top? Bottom? Left side or right side? What is a great composition? In my opinion it is an arrangement of shapes which, when put together in a certain order not only releases great visual energy, but also serves to lead the movement of the eye of the onlooker continuously around the picture surface.

I will attempt to show visually what I have discovered. As most pictures have four sides, because they are mostly rectangular, I have discovered that a composition on such a surface needs four elements or parts to it. These parts can be made to be very static and to imply no movement at all:

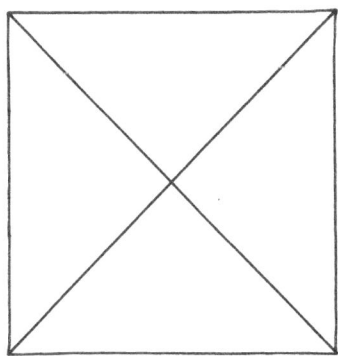

Or the same simple division can be used to achieve a feeling of great activity:

But this is not the only division into four parts applicable to a rectangle. Here is another:

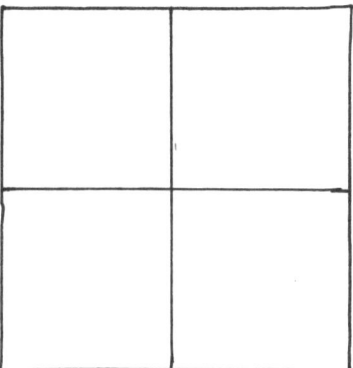

Because the parts are all off-centre they can create a differ-ent drama, disturbing the equilibrium:

Of course the rectangle doesn't have to be divided up into equal symmetrical parts like a flag. Also each part can merge into the next without any obvious join. Here is an example of an irregular division:

It would be possible to go on dividing a rectangle into four parts in many different ways but now we will break my rule and instead of four parts, try three:

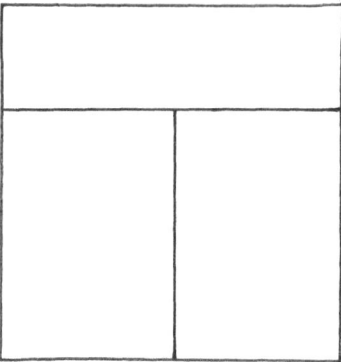

Or:

My personal view is that although this has equilibrium and some energy, it fails to lead the eye around the rectangle as successfully as the four part composition.

As a complete change here are five parts to the rectangle:

Which appear to revolve less successfully. They also fail to lead the eye around the rectangle. It is a more fussy arrangement, as if it has too many bits. No doubt in the hands of a fine and talented artist any rule can be broken successfully. In fact art, like science, is often concerned with breaking the rules of the past.

It can certainly be said that just one element, centralised, can be a successful composition as, for example, in the work of Mark Rothko, or with portraits of the head:

Perhaps this is because there are four spaces around the central shape, which naturally lead the eye around the rectangle.

It seems a much less successful composition if the main shape is placed off-centre.

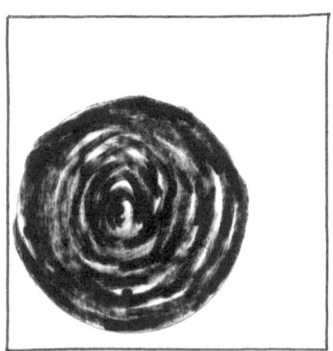

I have attempted to show that the four sides of the rectangle contribute to, if not control, the four-sided composition. The four parts within the picture work in partnership with the four edges of the rectangle, taking the eye on a continuous journey around the picture. A plain rectangular board, canvas or piece of paper needs a trigger to encourage this movement of the eye, if movement within the picture is required. One indicator of movement will not be enough. One arrow will not take the eye for a walk or a run around the picture and then return to its starting point:

Three arrows would hardly be sufficient:

Four seem to do the job much better:

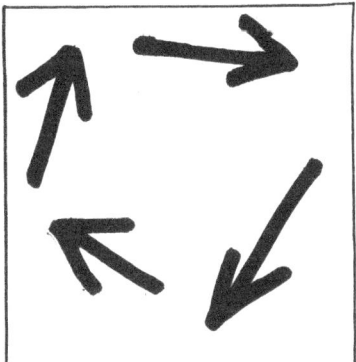

This is my approach, developed over a long period of experiment. Because it works for me doesn't mean that it will necessarily have a value for other artists, even though it might be a useful starting point for some. Nor will it be the secret with which to continually make successful paintings or drawings. That depends on the quality, clarity and intensity of vision.

There may be readable theories of composition and there may be schools and colleges of art which teach a sound basis in composition, but unfortunately I have come across none of these things, so I had to work one out for myself.

Country Runner 1

THE PURSUIT OF EXCELLENCE IN ART

I was asked the other day if I would talk to a room full of learned people about excellence in art. I nearly said yes when it struck me how very subjective art is. For instance, what I might consider to be excellent art someone else might hate. So do we have any criteria by which we might measure art, excellent or otherwise?

Let us first look at beauty. What is beauty? The French painter, Ingres, said, 'For something to be beautiful it has to have clarity and strength to avoid sentimentality.' For a long time I have thought that beauty (rather than prettiness) needed harmony and energy, but thinking about it, strength is a better word than energy because it allows for stillness as well as movement.

In the words of Leo Tolstoy,
' Beauty has nothing to do with virtue. Beauty is beauty, that is all.'

So beauty has no virtue built into it. A beautiful woman is not more loving, kind or compassionate than a plain one. A fine, harmonious building in Bath is not a better building than an ordinary one. It just looks good, that is all.

In fact, there have been times in history when beauty has been created while society had a callous indifference to goodness. The great age of English architecture in the middle of the eighteenth century was built at a time when the rich cared nothing for the poor, and women enjoyed anything but equality with men. There was little education for the less well-off. Power and influence was in the hands of a small number of wealthy people who enjoyed most of the privileges of life. Yet buildings in England have never been more harmonious in their design. Gardens were laid out with a great respect for nature, while silver and glassware, furniture and fabrics all reached an extremely high point in harmonious design and brilliant craftsmanship.

When people say truth is beauty – beauty is truth, I do not understand them. What has beauty got to do with truth? Beauty is a harmony of line, form, colour and composition combined with strength, that is all, whereas truth is what is, or what is perceived to be what is: a dustbin is a dustbin and is not beautiful just because it is one; there is more to beauty than that. And, anyway, it may only be perceived to be a dustbin. It may really be a bomb and not be a dustbin at all. So how we perceive things may not be the whole truth, verifiable on all counts.

The concept of truth in beauty and beauty in truth has been responsible for the most arid and tawdry periods of both architecture and art. Architecture after the Second World War, in the 1950s and 1960s was influenced by the theories of a group of designers given responsibility to build where bombs had destroyed. There was a pressing need for new houses and schools with a population re-establishing itself. The idea quickly and conveniently got around that, as long as something was functional – that a house sheltered people with basic comfort, air and light - then beauty had, hey presto, been achieved: walls and roofs for shelter, windows for light, doors for entry somewhere, all fed by the services of power, water and drainage. This was all, it seemed, an architect had to do. He had achieved the truth of a building, therefore he had achieved beauty. Strength and harmony were forgotten. In 1923, the celebrated Swiss architect, Le Courbusier had said, 'A house is a machine for living in.' It was overlooked after the war, in the hurry to build, that Le Courbusier had given a lot of thought to space, form and colour. But his example had not been properly followed.

Recent developments in art have taken the same course. If, for example, some bricks are placed on the floor, or some rubbish is attached to a canvas, because they are substances true to themselves, they must, we are encouraged to believe by some in the art world, be beautiful, so nothing more needs to be said. Everything is therefore beautiful and makes its own comment about itself, just by being itself. But I have never found this idea convincing.

Strength and harmony are forgotten. In order that this idea continues to make an impact, in the last gasp of the twentieth century bricks gave way to detroitus and rubbish was replaced by pickled corpses. This was to keep the public interested by shocking them, but it all makes the same point over and over again:

'What is itself is true, and can either be interpreted as beauty or, if you prefer, beauty, an outdated concept, has no place in art.'

Yet mankind is endlessly fascinated by beauty.

Is there a difference between beauty and prettiness? I believe there definitely is. Returning to Ingres' statement about strength and beauty, it could be said that prettiness is harmony without strength, such as a wedding cake, or a face which has an undistinguished bone structure but pleasingly placed features. I have often wondered why I find Walt Disney cartoons so unsatisfactory. I think it is because they are only pretty – the figures lack strength, being flattish without much form. The big-eyed faces and the bodies lack anatomical structure. I can find nothing in these creations to call beautiful, but some to call pretty. The presence of structure and strength gives an object a feeling of permanence – an unspoken knowledge that it could still be here in the future just as it has survived the past. This, I believe, is where beauty meets art.

It is surely impossible to make objective statements about excellent art created at the present time because there is always animated discussion about contemporary art. There are wounded sensibilities because styles and messages constantly change from what is established.

At the same time there are talents over-stating their case in order to be noticed, so it takes about twenty-five years for the dust to settle. But we can look back at any period of the past and make judgments about what is good and why.

What is art? What makes art different from design? I think we can only answer this by looking back and seeing what has survived by being considered great art. What has been most admired by people over long periods of time? Then we can see if anything links these works together.

If we take an over-view of art from its earliest known beginnings up to, say, 1980, I believe there is one common link which is inherent in excellent art of all periods: it always states,

'This is what it feels like to be human,' or, 'This is what I feel when I respond to this object or figure I have represented in my art.'

In the earliest cave paintings the representation of animals shows a knowledge, affinity and respect for them which would be hard to equal in any later period of art, even though styles became much more naturalistic. The question, 'What does it feel like to be a human being experiencing an animal,' has been answered thoroughly.

In Egyptian art, sculptors tell how it feels to be strong, serene and permanent. In Greek art, how it feels to be energetic and agile. The dramas of Christ's life are composed in line form and colour for the Church from around 1100 AD for at least five hundred years. But these are not just illustrations of events. Each great work shows what it feels like to be Christ because we know what it feels like to be us – to be human.

At the end of the nineteenth century there was a great burst of colourful and exuberant painting in France called The Impressionist Movement. Edouard Manet's 'Dejeuner sur l'Herbe,' showing a naked women having lunch on the grass with a group of clothed men, announced the beginning of Impressionism. It was painted in 1863. This sudden outpouring of artistic energy, re-examining nature in all its moods and seasons and how men and women fitted into this environment, continued persuasively for thirty years, exasperating its enemies and delighting its champions. Impressionism gradually gave way, after the paintings of Gauguin and Van Gogh, to Cubism and Expressionism.

But did Impressionism also answer the question I have posed as needing to be answered by all great works of art, 'What does it feel like to be human?' I believe it showed a harmony between mankind and nature more vividly than had ever been done in the history of art. Monet's gardens became so opened up to the artist's paint and brush that the viewer is lost in the scene. Van Gogh's toiling figures become part of the sun-dried grass. When he paints a sunflower or a Provencal chair he makes the painting tell us not only what he feels about those objects, but makes them tell us something of his own struggle with aloneness and survival.

In the great painting in London's National Gallery, (Kenneth Clark called it the greatest painting of the nineteenth century) Georges Seurat's 'Bathers at Asnieres' or 'La Baignade,'of 1884, this harmony between man and nature is slightly disturbed. Factory chimneys push smoke into the blue sky and, as the painter Francis Bacon remarked,

'It is the sort of grass you know is going to be built on.'

There is a feeling that the party between man and nature is coming to an end, and alienating forces are on the horizon. In this Seurat painting unease in the environment is contrasted with serenity (or resignation) of the figures as they sit with the composure of Egyptian sculpture.

I can go on at length attempting to prove the connection between great art and human feeling, but there is something more to say on the subject of design or 'beauty' in connection with art: Art is more than just design or decoration but cannot be disconnected from it entirely. The disowning of beauty in art has been attempted frequently in the twentieth century, but the works showing the greatest chance of survival admit harmony of design and strength of composition. As an example of this conjunction between beauty of design and the communication of what an artist feels about life, the work of Francis Bacon in the second half of the twentieth century shows the point powerfully. His work is often criticised as being too bleak and pessimistic about humanity, but at least it does speak loudly on the subject even if the message is unwelcome. What is frequently forgotten, however, is how much Bacon is conscious of the design and therefore the beauty of his canvasses. If a Francis Bacon painting is turned upside down making the subject matter less obvious, the beauty of the composition, line, form, colour and application of paint are all plain to see. If Bacon's work had not been executed beautifully he would not have enjoyed the huge reputation he did. He would have been relegated to the touchline alongside other ghoulish painters with joyless messages.

There are no absolutes in the study of this subject. Others find different purposes for art: pure entertainment or pure stimulation for instance. In my view excellent art needs to answer the question, 'How does it feel to be a human being?' and in answering this it needs to be, at the same time, fully aware of the construction of the design, otherwise called composition, and of the relationship between all its individual parts. When there is disharmony and discord it needs to be used to underline the feeling, not just to seek attention by shocking the viewer. Art is the genuine feeling of a human being told beautifully. Art is the making of a souvenir of life which says,

'I was here. I felt.'

These are the points which make art different from design. Art incorporates design, but design can exist without art. Art does not have to be liked by everyone who sees it, because not all art tells of perceptions we want to see or hear. Nevertheless, if the feeling is a true one and the work of art is put across with a sense of beauty, that is, with a fine sense of strength, line, form and colour, it may come to be regarded as excellent art. Time, alone, makes the final judgment.

The feelings that speak to us down the centuries are those experienced by each generation. The carriers of these sensory messages from one generation to another are works of art made by men and women called artists who, by applying themselves with body and soul, very occasionally make a sort of magic.

ART AND RELIGION

A long time ago, when I had drifted away from my early church and cathedral schooling, I used to say, when asked about religion, that I found all the spirituality I needed in art. If religion is about coming nearer to God by achieving a spiritual state, then that can be experienced by listening to a great piece of music, by hearing a great solo instrumentalist or by seeing a great painting. The artist has somehow bridged the gap between the mundane and the heavenly, replacing the anxiety of the moment with a momentary glimpse of all that is infinite. The awareness at these moments that certain human beings can create works of such power does, for a little while at least, inspire us with a feeling of the potential greatness of humanity. Some artists and performers can open the door to a more brilliant world. If we look at most of the great religions, how much do they rely on the artist to provide an environment and an atmosphere where a spiritual state of mind can prevail? The Christian cathedrals and churches with their stained glass, Buddhist and Hindu temples and Moslem mosques have all, from the earliest times encouraged the making of beautiful environments where the worship of God can be facilitated.

What happens when these works of art are taken away, or in the case of a new world religion, the Bahai Faith, where very little new art appropriate to the recognition of God has yet been developed? All that is left then is a sincerity of purpose; a conviction of the Faith's message, as was the case when the early Christians met in secret in unadorned rooms and in cellars. The Faith is kept going by the passionate believers. No beautiful aids for them, only single-mindedness. And yet, before long, they too are recognising, however unwillingly, the need for the arts to help them. Even if they learn this only by their lack of success in convincing others of their cause, they begin to call out,

"Where are the musicians to help us reach out to the world; where are the architects and artists to transform our places of prayer, and to attract people to us in their need for beauty?"

What is religion? "To know God and to worship Him?" If this is the case is it easier to do it in a community centre with EXIT signs and drawing-pinned notice boards, with fluorescent-tube lighting and spilt-on carpets, or is it more helpful to be in a space of beauty or even a place of emptiness, where the atmosphere in that place is of meditation and prayer?

If it does not really matter and if it is only the spirit of those present that is important, and not their surroundings, then humanity has been misguided in building temples, churches, mosques and cathedrals. There are small branches of faiths, for example The Plymouth Brethren and the Evangelical Fellowships which meet in school halls or in ordinary public rooms, but they do rely heavily on rousing songs and music to bring a feeling of uplifting praise to their gatherings.

If you follow an imaginary line through from these simple unadorned meetings ending up with sung choral evensong in one of the great cathedrals, surrounded with soaring architecture and medieval stained glass of infinite subtlety, the arts become progressively more prominent. In fact, in my opinion, the arts can end up being wholly the religion. The experience of praise and worship becomes very much a personal, individual experience, triggered largely by the art, architecture and music. The shared communal praise and worship is replaced by a private response to the arts and thereby a feeling of closeness to or "knowledge" of God is achieved.

Take this one step further. Take this same religious music out to a concert hall and play it with a spirit of reverence, and a similar feeling in the individual listener can be achieved. A glimpse of a reality much higher and greater than that of our daily ordinary experience.

Perhaps the truth is that the person who can come to know God in the unattractive community centre, and the one who needs architecture and art and music to help them are no better or worse than each other. They both achieve the same end: To know God and to worship him. There is only one thing missing if you leave the arts to do all the work without any community interaction, and that is the absence of a philosophy of how to lead your life; how to behave one to another; how to move the conduct of the world a little further towards kindness rather than savagery. I do not think that listening to Mozart and looking at a Giotto wall painting or even at Michelangelo's great works will necessarily make a sweeping contribution toward the greater humanity of man to man. As Tolstoy said: "Beauty has nothing to do with goodness. Beauty is beauty that is all." Beauty has to be associated with an outlook, a philosophy of behaviour which comes from outside itself, for it to make a real contribution to the more civilised behaviour of mankind. The art of the theatre which embraces all the other arts – music, dance, poetry, literature, painting and sculpture – can , at its very best, discuss, and even inspire progress towards an ever developing and increasingly humane civilisation. I have found in the theatre great moments of inspiration; of a spiritual rather than a material existence; a reminder that man or woman can, by a great magic, bridge that gap between earth and heaven while banqueting and satisfying all the senses. But in other hands theatre can just as easily be a degrading and degenerate experience. It depends on who is using the platform at any one time to communicate a philosophy. Unlike a religion the theatre has no ethical basis on which it is built – its ethics change constantly according to the piece being performed and to those who are creating it.

The newest world religion, The Bahai Faith, whose philosophy is the elimination of prejudice, the unity of all faiths, universal education and the equality of men and women, represents an attractive message to people at this time. This faith is gradually finding that the arts of music, poetry, literature, film, lighting, painting and dance – all ingredients of the modern theatre – are necessary to communicate this philosophy to the world. Baha'u'llah, the founder of the Baha'i faith has stated that the arts, crafts and sciences are of enormous importance in this current age. The arts are again weaving their essential spell as they have through thousands of years of history. This was well expressed by Shoghi Effendi:

'That day will the Cause spread like wildfire when its spirit and teachings are presented on the stage or in art and literature as a whole. Art can better awaken such noble sentiments than cold rationalising, especially among the mass of people.'

ARTISTS FOR GRANTED

I knew a mean professor once,
Who said he loved the arts.
Instead of buying books of poems
He photocopied parts.

I wrote this little ditty years ago when my aunt, Muriel Grainger, told me about an incident involving one of her poems. At her best she wrote powerful and concise poetry, publishing many collections, but earned almost nothing from it.

Now I'm not going to pretend that books of poems are, or even should be, on most people's Most Wanted List, but I am often saddened by the tiny monetary reward given to many creative people for the energetic contribution they make to a more colourful and interesting world. Artists can challenge accepted thought, or just create pure uncomplicated joy, but, either way, the world would be a much duller place without them: There would only be factual books to read in plain covers. No music, no paintings or drawings – only photographs. No harmonious colour, no theatre or entertainment, no cinema, no poems, rhymes, or stories and, how terrible, no stories for children. There would be work and there would be nature, but nothing of ourselves in between.

We say we believe in the arts – these creative diversions, these metaphors for life, but we really don't like to pay for them if we can possibly avoid it. Why? Well artists have fun don't they? If people are having fun why should they be paid? We forget there is no short cut to making something excellent. Years of commitment and practise are behind all worthwhile achievements. Anyone who has tried creating a handmade greetings card will realise how difficult it is and how long it takes to make something really good. It is not as easy as we imagine. It is this imagined easiness, combined with the idea that artists are always having fun, that leads people to ask them to work for nothing.

It is true that artists, working with words or music or pictures, mostly toil alone and, suffering many disappointments, are naturally keen to be used and recognised. They long to join the world of approved work; where they can be engaged in a project which makes them feel significant and wanted. So naturally those wanting to exploit them are aware of this and can very easily take advantage of it. The advantage-takers want to have the best quality work but their ambition is, if they can contact enough talent, to find someone to work for nothing, or next to nothing.

It is very unlikely though that they would expect this generosity of a doctor, a dentist, a banker, a lawyer or a builder. Why is this? I believe it is because these professions, and most others, are wise enough to present to the world images of genuine toil and serious endeavour which bear no resemblance to the easy fun the artist appears to be having.

Although I do realise the world will not soon be in a position to reward artists proportionately for their lifetime of creativity, I am very keen that any budget should be considerate, bearing in mind the thousands of hours of painful development which are essential for the perfecting of any skill. The real truth is that, generally, artists' lives are full of disappointments, set backs, and often isolation, with very little glamour attached. They should not be expected to work for nothing just because what they create seems more colourful, more exciting and occasionally more long-lasting than the apparent output from many other jobs. What a good artist creates is only compelling because of the total application he or she will bring to the task and their constant dedication towards learning how to do the work better.

This involves making mistakes and being in a constant mood of self training. Doctors and lawyers and bankers have to pay their bills, so do painters and writers and musicians. No-one should have a hand in starving those they say they believe in.

At a time when they were most successful, the group Pink Floyd used these memorable words at the very end of their great work 'The Wall':

> All alone, or in twos
> The ones who really love you
> Walk up and down outside the wall.
> Some hand in hand
> Some gathering together in bands,
> The bleeding hearts and the artists
> Make their stand
> And when they've given you their all
> Some stagger and fall, after all it's not easy
> Banging your head against
> Some mad bugger's wall.

Girl in a Landscape 1

EVOLUTION AND SO ON.
A CASE FOR GOD.

The evolution of all species is, nowadays, taken as a scientific certainty, and is only questioned, it seems, by religious fundamentalists, who prefer the Bible story of a flurry of activity, resulting in the creation of all that is.

I am not going to argue against the idea of a universe developing over twelve billion years or so out of the first atoms of hydrogen and helium, but I am always uneasy about the idea that anything can turn into something else of its own accord. The first atoms flying about in space, coming together to form other atoms – why? Why should they have any motivation at all to form anything else but themselves?

I cannot believe, as is often proposed, that conditions motivated change for the sake of survival. The universe was unbelievably hot. Atoms of hydrogen and helium did not, I believe, decide to come together in order to form other atoms in order to survive rather than perish. The theory of a constant 'survival of the fittest' must be applicable to the early universe as it said to be of the later. Otherwise there has to be a moment when the theory suddenly becomes applicable. When was that?

What difference would it have made if the universe had been extinguished like a damp firework after a very short time? There was no agenda for self-preservation built into an atom of hydrogen. Or was there?

After a million years or so the first stars were born out of swirling hot gases coming together, because the conditions were now right for matter to unite further. If the expansion had been too fast nothing could have formed; if it had been too slow everything would have collapsed back into itself.

The speed of the initial explosion was, Stephen Hawking states in 'A Brief History of Time', critically exact to one part in a hundred thousand million million.

Current thinking suggests that either this was all a happy accident, or that it is just the way the universe is – an automatic perpetual motion machine – expanding and contracting at critical speeds forever. Thus there is no need for a creative intelligence, they say, because it just does everything itself, like a clock that needs no battery or winding up; a universe which is and always will be creating itself and destroying itself. Exploding and imploding into infinity.

The critical speed of the big bang of creation could not have been a conscious decision of the original particles of matter. How would these particles know at what speed they should travel in order to ensure the eventual birth of stars, planets and life forms?

To me there is no other answer than that some form of higher intelligence was at work with a long-term objective; a vision of where all this apparent chaos was going to lead. I cannot believe in a universe which is in a perpetual cycle of creation and destruction for no purpose whatsoever. A big scientific joke. Sometimes an amusement park, sometimes an apocalypse, always without a theme.

As yet we know very little of this creative intelligence other than what we are told by the world religions. But the birth and development of the universe seems to come about in a way very familiar to anyone who has created anything: At first an idea, then a vision of the end result. Then chaos as the idea develops. Eventually, out of the apparent mess and piles of waste there comes a result which has a semblance of order, and, in time, a final resolution relating to, but not always identical to, the first idea. An evolution has taken place enabling the original idea to develop.

In the whole of this process nothing takes care of itself. No intelligence is busy in the workshop when you have left it, you have left it, nor does anything piece itself together. Without a creator all remains the same, and, if abandoned, the materials will deteriorate without fulfilling the purpose envisaged for them. They are not self-generating. They need a creative intelligence to be constantly at work for the plan to be realised.

Thus, a universe which goes its own sweet way makes no sense to me. I can only understand it as a process moving towards an objective resulting from an original idea. Nothing makes itself. It has to be made.

Returning to Stephen Hawking's 'A Brief History of Time', he refers to a phenomenon in physics called entropy. This means, broadly, that if things are left to themselves they assume a state of chaos. My understanding of this phenomenon is that if, for example, you put fifty children dressed in blue on one side of the playground and fifty in red on the other side, with a fence in between, then you removed the fence, very soon the reds and the blues would mingle in a disordered way. Never again would all the blues be on one side with reds on the other. Only if an intelligent influence intervened could a pattern be achieved – either by a teacher giving instruction, for example, or by one of the children taking charge. Only then could any kind of order be realised.

It was a thrilling moment for me when I read about this 'entropy' because for many years I had noticed how crowds appear to have a fairly even distribution of colour within them. Reds are dotted about all over the place, as are whites and all the other colours. Why, I always asked, do you not sometimes get a whole row of people dressed in blue? But you never do, unless of course they are influenced to dress alike with club colours for instance, or a uniform. Left to themselves things do not tend towards a pattern or order; they position themselves at random. It is the same with wild flowers in a field. In a natural state the flowers would be all over the place, colours mixed. Only if the gardener had sown seeds with a plan would there be any order instead of apparent chaos.

Leave things alone and they will surely go awry. Leave a house alone and it will quickly deteriorate. The roof will leak, the wood will rot, the bricks will fall out. Why should the universe be any different? Stephen Hawking says that, in his view, the universe is increasing in chaos, not the other way round. I profoundly disagree.

To start with an unimaginably hot explosion out of 'nothing' (or to be properly scientific about it – out of a singularity, when space and time do not exist because they are an infinitesimal point – and then, after twelve thousand million years of gases achieving sufficient structure to create, among many others, Johann Sebastian Bach with his music, Velasquez with his paintings, Shakespeare with his drama and beings capable of observing and theorising about the universe itself, surely takes a bit of intelligence somewhere along the line. Otherwise we have to believe they made themselves without a plan. And how do we know that there are not millions of other planets with other magnificently beautiful creations being made now at this very moment, or in the very near future. The universe could very well be moving away from chaos into a vast festival of achievement..

The more I think about it, and the more science I read (and I do read science in order to try to contradict myself) the more improbable it seems that anything makes itself, however long you wait. Creative intelligence is the fundamental guiding principle which gives birth to all that is made. Without it nothing is made, nor can anything develop into something else. Without creative intelligence all is chaos and disorder. Perhaps there will come a time when physics will recognise a new phenomenon called creative intelligence out of which will be derived an algebraic formula. But probably not yet.

TIME TRAVEL – A WARNING

When I heard it said that going back to a place where you spent a lot of time as a child can be painful I thought, 'Why painful? Those places don't belong to you anymore so the attachment is sentimental, and surely it's just a matter of making the worn out remark about how small everything looks now, when it seemed immense when you were a child.'

But I have recently experienced that it is certainly uncomfortable treading the exact ground and walking through the same rooms, almost unchanged for sixty years, where, for ten years I walked as a child. The word 'almost' is the key to the sadness because those two unavoidables: Time and Change have exerted their relentless power.

However exact the similarity between how things appear now and how we remember them, experiences cannot remain the same because time degrades them: Time peels paint, it removes roof tiles and uses spaces which were once welcoming bedrooms as dumping areas for unwanted belongings. Time rusts metal and covers rose beds with grass, and even when you may open a door and see an Art Deco bathroom which might appear exactly as it used to be, you soon realise it is not as it was at all. There are cupboards which shouldn't be there, made worse because they are the right style and period and seem to have the right qualifications, but they have entered in disguise, like uninvited visitors hoping not to be noticed. The marble statue of the boy on the window shelf is missing and where is my grandmother's yellow soap? And where have they put my small bed which was against the wall?

If Time is not enough to give you the feeling of being invaded, then Change will complete the experience. The unseen presence of all those who have affected that place with their contributions of change over the years is everywhere. Perhaps for the purposes of convenience, or for up-dating, or for stamping a personal taste onto an environment, Change ensures that nothing will stay the same.

The only territory where places, objects and people remain unchanged is in memory. Visiting the past in its present form can be disturbing because the changes that time has brought about seem like betrayals of our memory. The past which lives in the memory is pure and exact and true to itself and likes to stay that way, so, like a letter which has picked up tea stains, it can be spoilt by the foreign invasions which have taken place in later years.

So I suggest to anyone thinking of re-visiting territory belonging to the past: strengthen yourself. However often someone tells you, 'It's exactly as it was,' it certainly won't be, and it may be those tiny variations between how you remember it then, and how you find it now, which are the most unsettling. Remember that pilgrimages were made by travellers going to unfamiliar places belonging to others, not necessarily containing memories, they were not normally made to our own lands occupied by strangers.

CREATIVE CLUTTER
AND THE EXECUTOR
A letter to an elderly artistic relative

It strikes me, having recently helped to make some sense and pattern out of the creative work remaining after the death of an elderly relative, that artistic people have a responsibility to clear up their mess as they go along, so I feel driven to write this little reminder:

Dear Elderly Relative,

It is no good publishing and exhibiting and performing in your lifetime, seeking approval from others, and self-respect for yourself if, when you die, you leave all the less popular work in a big hopeful heap for someone else, usually a 'loved one,' to clear up. You are hoping, I am quite certain, that they will do what you failed to do in your lifetime: to magically have this work published, exhibited or performed. But what makes it any easier for your executors to do it now than it was for you to do when you were here?

You had thirty years of retirement in which to do it. If you were not going to scatter it out into the world yourself then surely you could have had it nicely typed and collated. A cover and a title on each piece would have been welcome too, with a date when it was done. Then at least one of your loving relatives or friends could have put it on a bookshelf to wait for the big day when the world was ready for it, or alternatively, they might just opt for the luxury of throwing it away. Drawers full of unsorted pages and muddled autobiographical bits and pieces will not do at all. You would not like it, I'm sure, if they were all chucked in the dustbin. You intended, I think you said,

'Something might be done with them.'

Do you realise that this means months of work for someone else to do? What were you doing during those thirty years of not going to the office?

Please do better in future.

Much love,

Me.

Of course we all know that most people leave clutter behind them when they die, but artists, whether writers, musicians, painters or sculptors, leave a special kind of hopeful clutter. They leave an invisible label on each piece of work saying,

'Don't throw this away if you love me.'

So we are left with masses of creative muddle to sort out, to make sense of and to feel we must keep.

Decisions eventually have to be made about what stays and what goes. Sweepings from the workshop seldom benefit anybody. Very occasionally, if the artist is very famous, the bits might be able to be sold to enrich the beneficiaries, but it is, in my opinion, a great arrogance to believe that what we leave behind – good, bad or poor, must not be destroyed. Some of it must, for the sake of space for those who are left.

It is much easier for artists themselves to sort out the good from the bad as they go along life's merry way.

I used to keep paintings from my earliest days. They were not, I felt, bad enough to be thrown away but, I had to admit, neither were they good enough to exhibit and sell. So they remained like hangers-on, following me from studio to studio, leaning against the wall, taking up valuable space as some were pretentiously large. Then came a studio fire in

November 1992 and the whole lot was burnt. I counted thirty five perished pieces of work in my memory. Records of my work were burnt also – card indexes and colour slides.

Most of these pictures I have not really missed very much, although it was upsetting at the time to think that I had little to show for the earlier years of work. So now I try to clean up as I go along. I do not destroy everything which does not sell; that would be over-dramatic, but after a while you come to know the weaklings; the pieces that do not speak back to you as you intended. So I keep the best and throw the rest.

As to my written efforts. Well, that is not so difficult. I will try to act on the advice I gave to the Elderly Relative and try to leave the stuff computer type-written with a title and in the order I intended. Then some kindly soul, whose awful job it will be to clear up my muddle will, for love, tuck the writings away on a shelf somewhere and say,

"Oh well, at least we don't have to read that lot before we sort it out."

Detail of Late Spring Flowers

FROM A PADDINGTON WINDOW

Looking down from the hotel window near Paddington Station, I saw the early morning people were on the move. Not in one direction but in many. Few were taking notice of anyone else, but all with some purpose or motivation for the movement in order to arrive somewhere eventually.

It would be easy to say they looked like ants in a colony, but to be honest, it was cockroaches that came to mind – a little more powerful and threatening than ants, and I was not far enough away for them to appear miniscule.

So what was their common purpose? Even though they appeared, and probably most of them wished to appear, individual and totally separate from each other, was that enough? It didn't appear to be so to me at that moment. Ants and cockroaches both go about their business for an ultimate common good. Can humans be so different as to live only for personal or small family benefit?

I felt, looking down on them from above, detached but not exempt, that they were, without having any idea of it, each one minutely part of a long-term plan – or a tiny sub-division of a mighty project – too large and far-reaching for each miraculous but specialised mind to conceive.